The Night Before the Fourth of July

To my uncle Warren and the Fourth of July
family gatherings that always involved fireworks—NW

To Flint and Mark, who kept me company
while the fireworks crackled and boomed!—AW

GROSSET & DUNLAP
Published by the Penguin Group
Penguin Group (USA) LLC, 375 Hudson Street, New York, New York 10014, USA

USA | Canada | UK | Ireland | Australia | New Zealand | India | South Africa | China

penguin.com
A Penguin Random House Company

Penguin supports copyright. Copyright fuels creativity, encourages diverse voices, promotes free speech, and creates a vibrant culture.
Thank you for buying an authorized edition of this book and for complying with copyright laws by not reproducing, scanning, or distributing any
part of it in any form without permission. You are supporting writers and allowing Penguin to continue to publish books for every reader.

Text copyright © 2015 by Natasha Wing. Illustrations copyright © 2015 by Penguin Group (USA) LLC. All rights reserved.
Published by Grosset & Dunlap, a division of Penguin Young Readers Group, 345 Hudson Street, New York, New York 10014.
GROSSET & DUNLAP is a trademark of Penguin Group (USA) LLC. Manufactured in China.

Library of Congress Cataloging-in-Publication Data is available.

ISBN 978-0-448-48712-0   10 9 8 7 6

The Night Before the Fourth of July

By Natasha Wing
Illustrated by Amy Wummer

Grosset & Dunlap
An Imprint of Penguin Group (USA) LLC

'Twas the night before July 4th
and all across the USA,
Americans were gearing up
for Independence Day.

Mom tied up the bunting
while I gave Dad a hand.
We hung up the flag
from our porch stand.

That night we both slept sprawled out in our beds,

while visions of fireworks popped in our heads.

The next morning, we dressed up in red, white, and blue.

I even wore stars, one on each shoe.

We lined up on Main Street.
Look! Here come the parade floats!

Hooray for the marching band!
And the 4-H club goats!

The mayor tossed candy.
I shouted, "Here! Here!"

An Uncle Sam walking on stilts
brought up the rear.

Friends and family came over for a backyard barbecue.
Dad fired up the grill as a storm started to brew.

The goodies were set
on the picnic table with care.
"Get 'em while they're hot," hollered Dad,
flipping burgers into the air.

"Grab the food!" shouted Mom . . .

and we raced through
the door.

In hot dogs! In salads! In blueberry pie!
In melon and corn! Keep those potato chips dry!

We gathered in the kitchen and spilled into the hall.
"Squeeze in!" said Mom. "There's room for us all."

As we munched on our food, Grandma turned to Grandpop.
"There'll be no fireworks show, if this rain doesn't stop."

"What?" we all shouted. No rockets' red glare?

Fourth of July without fireworks? That's totally not fair!

When what to our wondering eyes should appear:
With the rain suddenly stopping, the sky was now clear!

We piled in the car and drove to the park.
We threw down a blanket as it began to grow dark.

Dad lit the sparklers. We drew circles in the air.

We snapped glow sticks on our wrists and glow halos in our hair.

The first firework was launched
high into the night.
It bloomed like a flower,
exploding with light.

Whizz, crackle, BOOM!
"Woo-hoo!" cheered the crowd.
But my brother covered his ears
and whimpered, "That's too loud."

And now—the grand finale!
Wow! The best I'd seen yet.
A sky filled with color—
a show I'll never forget.

When the last firework fizzled like fairy dust in the sky,
we all cheered and shouted,

Happy 4th of July!!